To my writer friends Verla Kay, Linda Rodriguez Bernfeld,
and Ena Jones, who were with me when I wrote this book
at the Florida SCBWI conference

Also to my supportive husband, David
—L.J.S.

To my parents
—J.M.

little bee books

An imprint of Bonnier Publishing USA
251 Park Avenue South, New York, NY 10010
Text copyright © 2017 by Linda Joy Singleton
Illustrations copyright © 2017 by Jorge Martin
All rights reserved, including the right of reproduction in whole or in part
in any form. LITTLE BEE BOOKS is a trademark of Bonnier Publishing USA,
and associated colophon is a trademark of Bonnier Publishing USA.
ISBN: 978-1-4998-0278-8
Library of Congress Cataloging-in-Publication Data
Names: Singleton, Linda Joy, author. | Martin, Jorge (Illustrator) illustrator.
Title: A cat is better / by Linda Joy Singleton; illustrated by Jorge Martin.
Description: First Edition. | New York: Little Bee Books, (2017)
Summary: Picture book showing why cats are better pets than dogs.
Subjects: CYAC: Cats—Fiction. | Dogs—Fiction. | Pets—Fiction.
Classification: LCC PZ7.S6177 Cat 2017 | DDC (E)—dc23
LC record available at https://lccn.loc.gov/2016014968 | LCCN: 2016014968

Manufactured in China LEO 1116
First Edition
2 4 6 8 10 9 7 5 3 1

littlebeebooks.com
bonnierpublishingusa.com

A CAT IS BETTER

by
Linda Joy Singleton

illustrated by
Jorge Martin

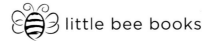

little bee books

CONGRATULATIONS!
I'm your new cat.
I'm the perfect pet for you.
You may take me home now.

Wait! Where are you going?
Do **not** pick up that dog.
A cat is better.

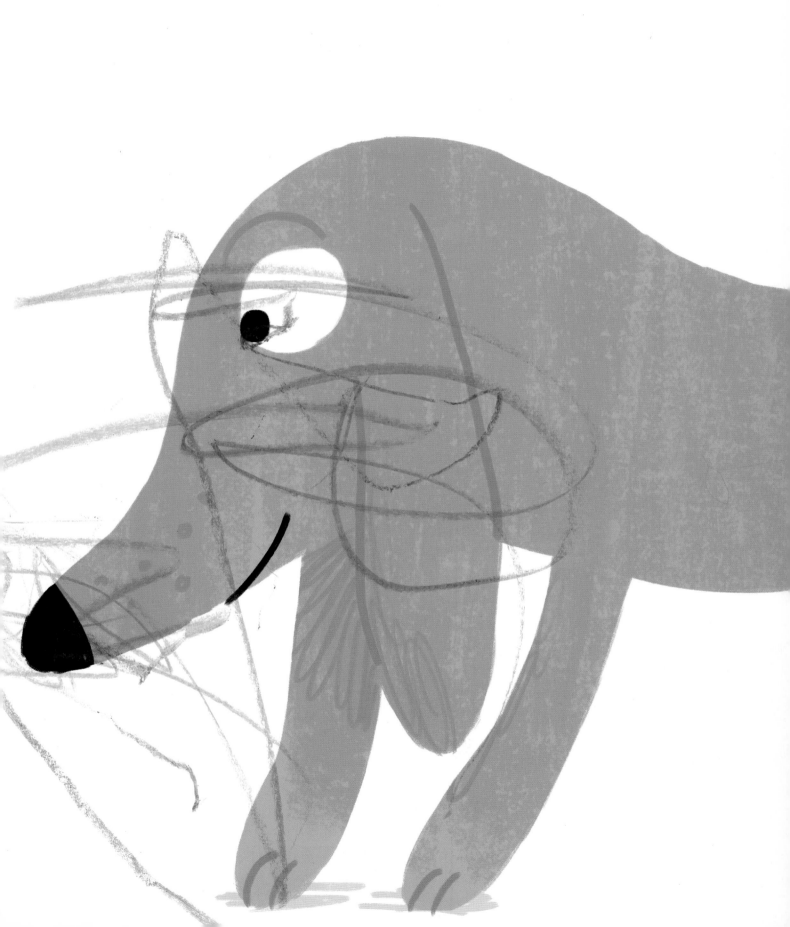

A cat is more elegant than a dog.

See how gracefully I leap?

Nice porch.

A cat is smarter than a dog.
No silly games of fetch.

I can
entertain
myself.

A dog yips and yaps and whines.
But a cat is musical.

Just listen
to my purrs.

PURRRRR

A cat is very well-behaved.
I will never pee on your floor
or chew your toys.

A dog gets
very, very dirty.

(Ugh. Dis-GUS-ting.)

No splashy baths for me.
I can lick myself clean.

YOWL! SPLAT!

I like being held.

Ooooooohh

A sparkly necklace for me?
Yes, I am beautiful.
Thank you very much.

But the dog isn't too bad.
I guess he can stay.
He can even keep the fancy bed.

ZZZZZ

But it's so quiet.

So very quiet.

And lonely.

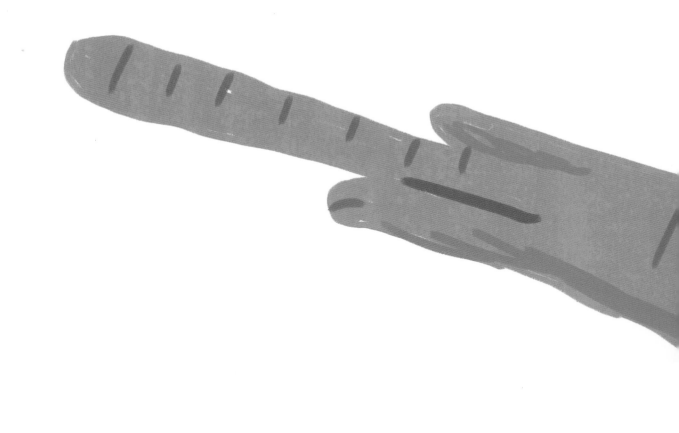

A cat is better
than a dog.

But sometimes
a dog can be...

Purrfect.